The Next Step

The Next Step

The Next Step

by

Beth Pollock

James Lorimer & Company Ltd., Publishers
Toronto

James Lorimer & Company Ltd. acknowledges the support of the Ontario Arts Council. We acknowledge the support of the Government of Canada through the Book Publishing Industry Development Program (BPIDP) for our publishing activities. We acknowledge the support of the Canada Council for the Arts for our publishing program. We acknowledge the support of the Government of Ontario through the Ontario Media Development Corporation's Ontario Book Initiative.

Cover design: Meghan Collins

The Canada Council | Le Conseil des Arts
for the Arts | du Canada

ONTARIO ARTS COUNCIL
CONSEIL DES ARTS DE L'ONTARIO

Library and Archives Canada Cataloguing in Publication

Pollock, Beth
        The Next Step / Beth Pollock.

(Streetlights)
ISBN 978-1-55277-441-0

        I. Title. II. Series: Streetlights

PS8631.O45A64 2009   jC813'.6   C2009-901676-1

James Lorimer & Company Ltd.,   Distributed in the
Publishers   United States by:
317 Adelaide Street West   Orca Book Publishers
Suite #1002   P.O. Box 468
Toronto, Ontario, M5V 1P9   Custer, WA U.S.A.
www.lorimer.ca   98240-0468

Printed and bound in Canada.

In honour of my parents,
Margaret Joyce and Paul Leroy Baker,
with love.

I gratefully acknowledge the Ontario Arts Council and James Lorimer & Company for their support through the Writers' Reserve program.

1

"Point your toes, Clara," Miss Tabitha said. "You're wearing ballet slippers, not army boots." Miss Tabitha was frowning again.

Clara tried to point her toes, but her feet still looked big and clunky, as if she were wearing boots.

Mama used to be a ballerina. When she danced, she looked like a swan. But when Clara saw herself in the mirror at the dance studio, she looked like a soldier. Everyone in a row doing exactly the same thing. Except Clara was usually a bit behind the others.

Miss Tabitha stepped back to talk to the whole class. Her dark hair was pulled tightly off her face and twisted into a bun. "Remember, next week we're measuring everyone for recital costumes. Don't be late!"

The recital! Clara's heart turned into a fist when she thought about the recital. She knew she wasn't good at ballet, and she didn't like dancing in front of an audience.

When Clara grew up, she wanted to be an inventor. She would invent really amazing things that nobody else had imagined. The first thing she'd make would be special ballet slippers that knew all the dance steps. Then she wouldn't worry about forgetting the routine.

The walls were covered in mirrors, and everywhere Clara looked she saw a reflection of Miss Tabitha frowning. Coming to class, Clara had hoped that Miss Tabitha would do something special for Valentine's Day, but there were no decorations or treats.

"Don't forget to practice your pliés," Miss Tabitha said. "Thank you, girls."

"Thank you, Miss Tabitha," the girls said in unison. They curtsied and scurried to the changing room. Jenny and Clara plopped down side by side on a bench.

"Wasn't Miss Tabitha grumpy today?" Jenny said, laughing. "Her ballet slippers must be two sizes too small!"

"I think she's Miss Crab-itha," Clara said, pulling her hair out of her ponytail.

Jenny didn't let mean people bother her. And she always tried to cheer Clara up after a bad class. Clara wished she was more like Jenny.

"Hey, I heard a funny joke. What's a pig's favourite ballet?" Jenny asked.

Clara shook her head.

"Swine Lake!" said Jenny.

Clara laughed. Being with Jenny was the only good thing about dance class. She wasn't sure if she and Jenny were best friends, but she hoped they were.

Clara tugged off her ballet clothes. Her body-suit was itchy and the straps bit into her shoulders. Off came her shoes, and then her tights. Last year she'd wanted to quit dance, but Mama had been so sick that Clara couldn't bring it up. Now, she felt confused about it. Everything at ballet reminded her of her mother. She remembered how Mama fixed her hair into a bun when she was little. And how Mama used to watch her through the dance class window. The only thing Clara had liked about ballet last year was how happy it had made Mama. Even when she was sick, she'd brought Clara almost every week and smiled at her through the window. Clara worried that if she stopped coming to dance class, maybe she wouldn't remember those things anymore.

If only it were easier to talk to Daddy. He was so sad when they talked about Mama that Clara hated to mention her, although she thought about her mother all the time. Someday she'd try asking him about ballet and he could help her decide.

A bossy voice came from the other side of the changing room. Ashley Mellor said, "How many valentines did you get, Stephanie?" Ashley and Stephanie were best friends, and they were the coolest girls in grade three.

"I didn't count," Stephanie said. "Lots."

"Me too," Ashley said. "I bet some kids didn't get as many as us. Mrs. Singh gave me a card that said 'You'd butter fly into my heart.' I'm going to hang it on the fridge when I get home."

Mrs. Singh was Clara's third grade teacher at school. Ashley and Stephanie sat at Clara's table.

"She gave me that one, too," Stephanie said.

"She had another card that said 'Bee my valentine.' She gave it to the kids she doesn't like. All it had was a stupid bee."

Ashley glanced at Clara. Clara was glad that her 'Bee my valentine' card was stuffed in her backpack. She wondered if Ashley had seen her card at school.

Clara and Jenny pulled their coats off the hooks and scrambled out of the changing room. Clara's nanny, Tess, always picked them up after class. Tess didn't notice them coming out, because she was trying to stop Clara's brother Calvin from yanking the books off the shelf.

"Hi, Tess," Clara said.

Tess twisted around, still holding Calvin by one arm. "Hi, girls! Calvin wants to read seventeen books at once. Wait a sec while we put them back."

Being in the waiting area was the worst part of dance class. Last September, Clara had forgotten for just a minute that Mama wasn't there. She'd come running out of class and stood in the doorway, scanning the room for Mama. It hadn't been until she'd noticed Tess that her stomach had caved in, and she'd remembered Mama wouldn't be there again. Now, her face turned red, thinking how she'd stumbled back to the changing room that day, eyes filling with tears.

Tess and Calvin finished stacking the books and Calvin ran over. He was wearing his snowpants, and he rustled as he ran across the room. He threw his arms around Clara's neck and squeezed so hard she almost fell over.

"That hurts!"

"Hug Clara," he said.

"That isn't hugging, that's tackling." Calvin was only two, but sometimes he ran at Clara like a tiny football player.

Tess took his hand. "Wait 'til he's as big as

you, Clara. Then we're all in trouble."

Calvin was a pest sometimes, but Clara didn't think he'd ever really be trouble. Ballet class — and how to talk to Daddy about it — were trouble enough.

2

Does she remember? Clara wondered as she sketched roses on the last page of her math workbook.

Every year, the kids in Mrs. Singh's class invited their mothers to school the week after Valentine's Day. They served cookies and lemonade and gave them a tour of the classroom.

Maybe Mrs. Singh didn't remember that Clara didn't have a mom. Maybe she thought Tess brought her to school because Clara's mom had an important job. Jenny's mom was a lawyer and Clara hardly ever saw her. Maybe Mrs. Singh thought Clara's mom was a lawyer.

"Mrs. Singh," Ashley said, "Clara isn't listening."

Clara sat up quickly, covering her doodles with her arm.

"We can all be in charge of our own listening," Mrs. Singh said. "I think Clara heard me say we're having Special Friend Day next week. You can invite your mother or father, one of your grandparents, your nanny, or a friend. The important thing is that you invite someone you love."

"Last year you called it Mom's Day," Ashley said. "I like that better than Special Friend Day."

"Ashley, you may invite whomever you want this year. You may choose to invite your mother, or you may choose someone else."

Mrs. Singh gave Ashley her famous look that said, "*This* conversation is over."

"We'll have the party before school, and your friends may stay until the morning bell rings. Please think about who you'll invite. We'll make our invitations tomorrow."

Clara glanced around the room at the Valentine's Day decorations left from yesterday's party. Some were starting to sag. A huge red heart at the back of the room was so droopy, Clara saw the masking tape loop on the back.

Of course Ashley would bring her mom. Clara saw Ashley's mom at the school every day. Clara loved the little white tennis outfits that Mrs. Mellor wore when it was warm. They were cute and clean. Clara wished she could wear little white tennis outfits, too.

"It's almost dismissal time, boys and girls. Please tidy your desks and get ready to go." Mrs. Singh stopped at Clara's table. "Thank you for the lovely valentine picture you painted, Clara. When I took it home and showed Mr. Singh, we agreed that you're a talented artist."

Clara blushed. "Thank you." She'd wanted to do something extra for Mrs. Singh.

"She's the best painter in the class," Jenny said as Mrs. Singh moved to the next table.

The bell rang. It was Jenny's turn to wipe off the whiteboards, so Clara followed Ashley and Stephanie out the door by herself.

"I'm inviting my mom next week. What about you?" Stephanie asked.

"Me too," Ashley said. "I don't care what Mrs. Singh says. It's really Mom's Day. It would be stupid to bring anyone else."

Clara didn't want to hear any more. She jerked open her locker, yanked on her coat and boots, and ran out to the yard. Far away, Tess was waving at her from the corner of the parking lot.

"Let's scoot!" Tess called. "Calvin missed his nap today and he's very cranky."

I'm cranky, too, thought Clara. She shuffled through the snow, letting her footprints snake into two long ribbons. *I hate Special Friend Day.*

Calvin was crying and kicking the snow in the parking lot. Tess held his hand tightly as they walked to the car. Tess had three studs in each ear that looked like rubies, and her hair was super-short and dyed to match the studs. When Clara grew up, she wanted to look like Tess.

But today, she just wanted Calvin to stop crying.

When they got home Clara put her things away, and went to the kitchen table where Tess was setting out cheese and crackers. Calvin grabbed all the crackers on the plate and set them in front of himself.

"Don't be a pig," Clara said.

Calvin lay on top of the food and spread his arms out to the sides.

"Snack is for both of you," Tess said. "Please share it with Clara."

Clara heard some of the crackers crumbling under his chest.

Tess lifted him off the table. Bits of cracker were sticking to his sweater. Some of them fell to the table as he kicked and squirmed.

"Quiet time for you," Tess said, carrying Calvin out of the kitchen.

Clara made a face at the pile of crumbs. The ones that weren't broken were covered in sweater fluff. She went to the cupboard and got out the chips.

As she ate her snack, Clara thought about Special Friend Day. Jenny, Ashley, and Stephanie would bring their moms. Olivia would bring her stepmother. Was Ashley right? Was it stupid to bring anyone other than your mother?

Who would Clara invite?

If it was Special Friend Day, she had to choose a special person. Daddy? No one was better than Daddy. But Clara didn't feel right about asking him, because that would make him think about Mama. He would be the only dad there and that might make him feel lonely. She wouldn't bring Calvin, either. He'd probably eat all the cookies and knock over the lemonade. Aunt Bridget lived too far away. Tess? Clara wondered about inviting her, but it didn't feel right. She was afraid that people might think that Tess was her mother. She loved Tess, but nobody would ever take Mama's place.

Tess and Calvin came back in the kitchen. Calvin was holding his teddy bear, Poppy, in his left arm and had a soother in his mouth. He didn't look happy, but at least he wasn't crying.

"I'm going to read to Calvin," Tess said, wiping off the kitchen table. "Got any homework?"

"Just spelling," Clara said. She had math homework too, but if Tess knew, then she'd make Clara do it. She didn't feel like doing math.

"You can work on it before dinner." Tess and Calvin went into the living room. Clara pulled the spelling homework out of her backpack and sat on one of the big wooden chairs at the table. She decided to stop thinking about Special Friend Day. It was giving her a stomach ache.

* * *

Clara had finished her spelling and was playing in her room when she heard the front door open.

"Daddy!" she yelled, running to greet him.

She reached the door at the same time as Calvin, and Daddy hugged them both.

"How are you guys?" he asked.

Calvin wedged his elbow against Clara's hips to get more room with Daddy. Clara elbowed him back and Calvin started to cry.

"No fighting, you two, I just got home. Something smells good in the kitchen. Are we having Thai chicken tonight?"

Tess was standing at the kitchen door, laughing. "If Calvin stops bouncing around long enough to let me get it on the table."

Tess made good chicken, but it wasn't crispy

like Mama's. Clara wished Tess made plain fried chicken from Mama's recipe.

"Tell you what," Daddy said. "How about the three of us go in the living room while Tess finishes up."

Daddy took each of them by the hand. They went in and sat on the couch.

"Calvin, I bought you some new jeans today. If you don't stop putting your knees out, I'll have to buy a jean factory!"

Clara would have liked new jeans. She wondered why Daddy hadn't bought her some, too.

While Calvin told Daddy about the games he'd played, Clara heard Tess moving around the kitchen. Clara always set the table, but today she was hoping that Tess would do it for her.

"Clara, come and set the table please," Tess called.

Clara pretended she didn't hear. Daddy ruffled her hair.

"Better go and help," he said. "We'll have time together later."

Clara slid off the couch and stomped out to

the kitchen. No fair. She wanted to be with Daddy too. Daddy was late because he was buying jeans for Calvin. Rotten Calvin got to talk first, and now he had Daddy to himself.

She grabbed the utensils and slammed them around the table. She picked up the butter dish and banged it down too.

"The glasses are on the counter. Please pour the milk."

Clara took the milk pitcher from the fridge and thumped it on the counter. Milk sloshed all over.

"You know where the paper towels are."

Clara ripped off two towels and wiped the counter. After she finished pouring the milk, she was dying to bang the glasses on the table, but that would only mean more wiping.

She made it through dinner with no more spills. After Tess left for her night course, Daddy got Calvin ready for bed. Calvin didn't even try on his new jeans. He was asleep before Daddy finished the lullaby.

Clara put on her pyjamas, struggling to do up

the buttons. A minute later, Daddy knocked on her bedroom door.

"Come in!" she said. She moved to the far side of the bed, making room for him to sit next to her, his head against the wall.

"How was your day?" he asked.

"Okay, I guess," Clara said. "We're having Special Friend Day next week. Last year it was called Mom's Day."

"Oh," Daddy said. His eyes fell.

Clara rushed to keep talking so he wouldn't look sad. "Mrs. Singh told us we could invite anyone we want. But Ashley said it would be stupid to bring anyone but your mom."

"Do you care what Ashley thinks?"

"N-no." Clara did care what Ashley thought, but she didn't know why.

"If somebody is a true friend, they don't say things that are unkind to you," Daddy said. "Friends stick up for each other."

She remembered how Jenny had said she was the best painter in grade three. "How do you know if someone is your best friend?" she asked.

"It's easy to know if someone is your good friend," Daddy said. "A good friend treats you with kindness. A good friend feels sad for you when you're sad, and helps you celebrate when you're happy."

She watched the shadows glide across her bedroom wall as a car drove down the street. Jenny was definitely a good friend. "But how do you know if someone is your *best* friend?"

"Being best friends happens slowly. You can't make someone be your best friend. But if you spend a lot of time with them, and have fun together, and look after each other, then ... maybe you'll be best friends."

Clara took a deep breath. Daddy was usually busy, and didn't have much time to talk about important things. It was hard to tell him about her problems. But now he was here with her, without Calvin butting in. Time to ask him about dance.

"Daddy?" she said.

"Uh-huh?"

Clara crossed her fingers on both hands. "I

know you like me being in ballet. And Mama loved my recitals. But the thing is — I'm not good at ballet. Miss Tabitha is mean, and I never remember what I'm supposed to do next." She paused.

Daddy didn't say anything.

"Daddy?" Clara whispered.

He let out a little breath, like half a snore. Clara sighed. Mama had always listened to her at bedtime, and didn't fall asleep. Would Daddy ever be able to help her like Mama did?

3

"Eight times six ... Clara, can you tell us what eight times six is?"

Clara had been staring out the classroom window. She'd forgotten that she was in math class. She was watching the kindergarten kids build snow castles and forts. The suncatchers Clara's class had made last month still hung in the window, sparkling in the light.

When Clara heard Mrs. Singh call on her, she thought as fast as she could.

"Eight times six ... uh, forty-six?"

A couple of kids laughed.

"Clara, please pay attention to the lesson. Ashley, can you answer the question?"

"Eight times six is forty-eight," Ashley said triumphantly.

Clara's face went hot. She tried to focus on the lesson, but math was boring. Daddy had helped her practice multiplying on the weekend. She didn't remember any of it. Math was almost as bad as dance class. But at least Mrs. Singh was nice.

"Girls and boys, I'm handing out multiplication sheets for you to work on," Mrs. Singh said. "Please keep your eyes on your own work."

Clara sighed. She held her face in her hands and squished her mouth up to make fish lips at the page. She wrote, "I hate math" in black letters at the top of the page. Then she remembered the sheet was going back to Mrs. Singh. She tried to rub it out but the letters were too dark, so she scribbled over them instead.

5 x 4. Five groups of four. Clara didn't have that many fingers. *5 x 1 = 5*, she thought, *5 x 2 = 10, ... I wish Ashley was in the other class, no I wish she went to another school, 5 x 3 = 15, so 5 x 4 = ... 20!* She wrote it down.

If only she'd done her math homework last night. Today's multiplication sheet might be easier.

Clara wished she could invent a magic pencil that would know all the answers to math questions. She'd hold the pencil and it would skim across the page. If Clara invented a magic pencil, she'd get an A on every math test.

Clara peeked over at Stephanie's page. She was halfway down the first column.

"Mrs. Singh, Clara's cheating," Ashley said.

Mrs. Singh walked toward them. "I'm *not* cheating," Clara said.

"Oops, I guess not," Ashley said. "Stephanie and I have the *advanced* worksheets. You have the easy one."

"No more talking, girls," Mrs. Singh said quietly. "Keep your eyes on your own work. And don't compare your work to anyone else's."

As the teacher walked back to the front of the class, Ashley smiled at Clara. Not a friendly smile, but a smile that said, "I caught you." Maybe even, "I'm smarter than you."

Clara tried to ignore her and looked back at her work. She heard paper rustling. Someone had already moved on to the second page!

She struggled through the questions. When the recess bell rang, she was only partway down the first page.

"Boys and girls, bring your math sheets to my desk before you go out." When Clara took her sheet to the front, Mrs. Singh said, "Could you wait at your table, please? I'd like to talk to you for a minute at recess."

Did Mrs. Singh think she'd been cheating? Clara felt sick. She would never, ever copy somebody else's work, even if she hadn't done the homework. What if Mrs. Singh didn't believe her? Clara loved her teacher, and couldn't bear it if Mrs. Singh thought she had cheated.

After the other kids were gone, Mrs. Singh sat down in the chair beside Clara.

"I wasn't cheating!" Clara said. "Honest, I wasn't!"

Mrs. Singh looked surprised. "Of course you weren't. I trust you to do your own work."

Clara squirmed as she thought about last night's homework.

Mrs. Singh cleared her throat. "I wanted to remind you that you're welcome to bring anyone you want to Special Friend Day. Invite someone who you care for."

Mrs. Singh must remember she didn't have a mom. Clara said, "Some of the kids said it would be dumb to bring anyone but their moms."

"Then some of the kids are wrong. We'll make our invitations after recess, and I will welcome any friend of yours."

"Okay," Clara said.

Mrs. Singh smiled. "Now run along and catch up with your friends."

Clara trudged to her locker. Maybe she'd make an invitation and decide later who to give it to. Or maybe she'd throw it out and pretend to give it to someone. But then what would she do on Special Friend Day?

She didn't want to think about it now. She pulled her coat on and ran out the door. Everyone was already playing — where was Jenny?

Ashley and Stephanie were leaning on the fence, laughing and talking. Stephanie waved at Clara, but Ashley pretended not to see her.

Clara definitely didn't want to go over to them. Ashley was probably talking about how only the losers wouldn't bring their moms. But Clara didn't want to stand by herself in the middle of the playground either. She scanned the playground for Jenny and when she realized she wasn't there, her stomach caved in. Sometimes Jenny went to the library at recess. Clara could check there, but she didn't think the teachers in charge would let her back into the school at recess. She kicked the frozen ground, pretending that she actually wanted to be standing by herself in the playground. Clara's eyes filled with tears, and she brushed them away with the back of her mitten.

When she looked up, she saw a bunch of girls playing freeze tag by the side of the school. Kerry, Lexy, and Olivia were racing around — and Jenny was there, too!

Clara ran over, but stopped halfway across the

field, not sure if she should join them. Then Jenny saw her.

"Clara!" she shouted. "I need you to set me free!" She waved at her from beside the climbers.

"I'll save you," Clara called. She touched Jenny to free her, then screamed as Lexy almost tagged her.

When the bell rang, Clara ran into the line with the other girls. And she suddenly realized who she could invite to Special Friend Day.

*　*　*

Mrs. Singh had set paper and pencil crayons on the tables for students to create their own invitations. Clara took extra care with hers — the colouring was tidy, the printing was small. She wrote her name — Clara Cooper — at the bottom of the invitation. She didn't let anyone see it. She decided she'd deliver it after school.

When the bell rang at 3:30, the other kids ran out into the crowded hall. Clara hung behind, straightening her desk.

"Be a dear, Clara, and sharpen a few pencils for me?" Mrs. Singh said.

Clara loved sharpening pencils for Mrs. Singh. She made sure they were perfect, not so sharp they would break the first time someone used them. She wanted to do a great job for her teacher.

Would Mrs. Singh be Clara's special friend?

Clara bit her lip and handed the invitation to her teacher.

"This is lovely, dear. Who will you give it to?"

"You."

Mrs. Singh looked puzzled for a second. Then she leaned over and smiled at Clara. When she answered, her voice was even softer than usual.

"Are you inviting me to be your guest?"

"Yes," Clara said.

Suddenly she realized what a dumb idea it was. Mrs. Singh couldn't come with her. She had to pour lemonade and greet people at the door. Why had she invited Mrs. Singh? If only she'd thrown out the crummy invitation and pretended to be sick on Special Friend Day. Clara wanted to grab the invitation back and run out of the class.

Mrs. Singh knelt down to face Clara. "What

an original idea!" she said. "I've never been invited to Special Friend Day before."

Mrs. Singh had said it was a good idea, but she hadn't said yes. Clara felt all mixed up. Even though she wanted Mrs. Singh to be her Special Friend, she worried that she was asking something that was all wrong. "You have to pour lemonade. I guess you'll be too busy to come with me."

"I would love to be your guest. Now I have a perfect excuse not to pour lemonade," Mrs. Singh said. "I'll ask Mr. Hahn to help serve drinks."

Clara couldn't believe it. Mrs. Singh would ask the principal to help so she could be Clara's special friend!

"Thank you, Mrs. Singh!" Clara said, and ran out into the hallway.

She burst out of the school. Most of the kids had left already and only a few stragglers were waiting in the yard. The snow was coming down hard. Clara looked around and saw Tess and Calvin waiting for her over by the climbers. Calvin was trying to kick his boot off and Tess was trying to keep it on.

Clara was just about to run over to them when Ashley stepped in front of her. "I heard what you said to Mrs. Singh," Ashley said. "You can't be her special friend. She's everybody's friend."

Clara blinked but didn't say anything.

Ashley continued. "Teachers aren't allowed to have favourites. I'll tell my mom to complain to the principal." And with that, Ashley flounced off to her mom's car.

Clara plodded over to meet Tess and Calvin. Of course Mrs. Singh would be her special friend ... Wouldn't she?

4

Clara peered out her bedroom window. It had snowed a ton during the night and the roads hadn't been ploughed yet. Waves of sparkling snow drifted almost as high as the window.

When she got to the kitchen, her dad was reading the newspaper while Calvin crouched beside him and drove his bulldozer into Daddy's chair leg.

"Where's Tess?" Clara asked.

"The roads aren't safe to drive yet. Too much snow. Tess can't get here."

"How will I get to school?"

"School's been cancelled. I'm staying with you today."

A snow day with Daddy! "I'm going to build a snow fort," she said. "I'm going to make a hundred snowballs and get Calvin good!"

"First you can eat some breakfast," Daddy said. "We'll go out together when you've eaten."

Clara was so excited about getting outside, she could hardly finish her cereal.

After breakfast, Daddy said, "I'm going to shovel the driveway. Will you guys come to the front yard with me?"

"Yahoo!" said Clara.

"Yahoo!" said Calvin.

"Clara, can you help Calvin get dressed? It's cold outside. You'll both have to bundle up."

Clara held Calvin's hand and led him to his bedroom. Daddy had already changed Calvin's diaper — Clara didn't do diapers — so she got his clothes out. Sometimes Calvin fidgeted, but today he was good. He wanted to get outside in a hurry.

"Run out and help Daddy in the kitchen," Clara said when Calvin was ready.

"No," he said, "I help Clara."

If only her little brother would do what she asked. But she felt sad for him because she didn't think he remembered Mama. Even though Clara missed Mama terribly, at least she remembered her. Clara guessed Calvin didn't even have that. So, sometimes, she let Calvin get his way. "Don't touch *anything*," she said. They both went into Clara's room and she got dressed. He played with one of her stuffed animals, but he didn't touch anything else.

Once they had their coats and boots on, Clara and Calvin ran outside. He'd wanted to bring Poppy, but Clara had said his teddy bear would be too cold without a coat. So Calvin had propped up Poppy in the living room window to watch them.

Calvin had brought his red pail outside. He filled the pail with snow and dumped it on the ground.

"Can I play with you?" Clara asked.

Calvin nodded. But when Clara came over, he held his pail tightly to his chest. "My pail," he said.

"Okay," Clara said. "I'll help you fill it."

Calvin didn't mind Clara helping him fill the pail, as long as he held it and dumped it himself. She helped him about a dozen times, but grew tired of it. Eventually, Clara wandered to the end of the driveway to talk to Daddy.

"Do you remember the snow day last winter?" Daddy asked as he shovelled around the car.

Clara giggled. Last year, it had snowed too hard on Valentine's Day to go to school. At first, Clara had been disappointed because she didn't want to miss the school party. But that snow day had been Clara's best Valentine's Day ever. Mama and Tess had planned a Valentine treasure hunt in the morning. Then in the afternoon, while Calvin napped, they'd baked heart-shaped cookies with Clara. They'd all laughed when Tess pretended to sneak some batter when no one was watching.

Then Clara stopped giggling. She remembered Mama's white face. Mama had worn a red-and-gold kerchief that day. Clara remembered because it matched the red hearts they had hung around the house. Mama had a whole drawer full of kerchiefs that she wore after her hair started to fall out. Even with no hair, Mama was the prettiest mother in the world.

Clara remembered how Mama wanted to touch her all the time. Mama kissed her hair, her hands, her face. When Clara closed her eyes, she still tasted Mama's kisses.

A wet snowflake hit her face. She opened her eyes and saw Daddy leaning on the shovel, watching her.

"Are you okay?" he asked.

"I guess so," she said.

"It's hard, isn't it?"

Clara nodded. She ached to talk about Mama, to tell Daddy how she missed her every day. But Daddy had that sad look on his face. If she talked about Mama, it might hurt both of them. She said nothing.

A voice down the street called, *"Claaa-raaa!"* Jenny was wading through the snowdrifts toward the house.

"Isn't this great?" Jenny lived on Clara's street, half a block away.

Daddy went to the end of the drive to wave to Jenny's dad, Mr. Suzuki, who was shovelling too.

"Want to build a snowman?" Jenny asked.

"Yeah!" said Clara.

"Yeah!" said Calvin.

"How 'bout you build a little snowman, and Jenny and I will build a big one beside it?"

Calvin beamed. He dropped to his knees and started to heap the snow together in a mound.

The snow was deep, and Jenny and Clara both got some in their boots. Clara's socks were cold and wet but she was having so much fun it didn't matter. She flexed and pointed her toes to keep them warm. Then she remembered what Miss Tabitha had said about pointing her toes.

"Miss Tabitha was really mad the other day," Clara said.

"She's always mad about something," Jenny said.

"Do you like ballet?" Clara asked. She knew that Jenny took jazz on Thursdays, as well as ballet on Tuesdays with Clara.

Jenny shrugged. "I like jazz better. The

costumes are better, the music's better, and the teacher's way better."

"What song is your jazz class dancing to for the recital?" Clara asked.

"'Hakuna Matata'." The theme of the recital was *The Lion King*, and all of the classes were dancing to a song from the movie. "Miss Erin is so great. At the end of every class, she plays the song once for fun. We can sing it and even act it out if we like."

"Wish I was in jazz instead of ballet."

"You could switch next year."

"Ballet was so important to Mama. She liked bringing me to class and watching me in the recitals. I don't know if it would be right to quit."

"She wouldn't want you to keep taking something you hated."

"I know. But I'm afraid to ask Daddy about it."

"Why?"

"Because every time he thinks about Mama, he looks like his heart is hurting."

Clara glanced at Calvin's snowman. It was still just a small pile of loose snow.

"Can I help you?" she asked.

Calvin nodded, and she and Jenny started rolling balls for the body.

Some tree branches had fallen down with the storm. Clara gathered them and stuck them in the snowmen's sides for arms. When they finished their snowmen, the girls stood back to inspect their work.

"Get a couple of hats and they'll be perfect," Jenny said.

Clara went in the house and found some extra hats. She got buttons from the button bag for eyes. She even brought out a Toronto Maple Leafs stick flag from the living room.

She ran outside and they stuck the hats and buttons on the snowmen.

Calvin poked the flag in his snowman's arms. "Go, Leafs, Go!" he said.

"These are the best snowmen ever!" Jenny said. "Now we have to give them names."

"Calvin," Calvin said, pointing at his little snowman.

"Calvin?" Clara laughed. "Why do you want

to call it Calvin?"

"He gots my hat."

Jenny laughed too. "Okay, then this one has to be Clara. Clara Cooper the Second." She paused. "What's your middle name?"

"I don't have one," Clara said.

"Doesn't everyone have a middle name?"

Clara shook her head.

"Then I'll give you one," Jenny said. "How about Aiko? It's my cousin's name. It means 'loved one' in Japanese."

Clara smiled and said, "That's a pretty name." Jenny must really like her to call her Aiko.

"Are you bringing your dad to Special Friend Day?" Jenny asked.

"I wanted to bring a girl, so I'm inviting Mrs. Singh."

"Great idea! But won't your dad feel left out?"

Clara hadn't thought of that. Would Daddy's feelings be hurt that she chose Mrs. Singh? Clara felt her stomach ache again. "Anyway, I don't know if she can come. Ashley said Mrs. Singh isn't allowed to be one person's special friend, and her mom's going to complain to the principal."

Jenny rolled her eyes. "Ashley always says her mom's going to see the principal. Don't listen to her."

"Why doesn't she leave me alone? She isn't mean to you."

Jenny shrugged. "You let Ashley get to you too much. She used to be mean to me, but I ignored her. And she stopped."

"Every time she talks to me I get mixed up and say dumb things."

"Forget about her. You're nice, and she isn't. Everyone else likes you."

Clara was happy to hear that, but she was afraid that ignoring Ashley wouldn't be that easy. "Anyway, I'm wearing my blue dress for Special Friend Day," Jenny said. "Mom said I had to wear a dress. What are you wearing?"

"My pink dress with white roses." Mama had bought it for her last year, and it had been big on her, so Clara knew it would still fit. If Mama couldn't go to Special Friend Day, then at least the dress Mama gave her would go.

Daddy leaned his shovel in the snow bank and called across the yard. "Jenny, why don't you ask your father if you can have lunch with us?"

"Sure!" Jenny said. "I'll be right back."

Clara walked her to the end of the driveway.

"Tess made chocolate cake yesterday, and there's lots left for dessert," she said.

"I love her chocolate cake. Remember when she made it for your party? You're lucky she's your nanny. She makes the best chocolate cake ever."

Clara stiffened. Tess's cake was good, but Mama had made the best chocolate cake ever. Mama used to cover her cakes with confetti candy. The last time she had made cake, there were so many sprinkles that Clara could barely see the chocolate icing.

Clara watched Jenny plod down the street. Yes, she was lucky to have Tess. But she'd rather have Mama.

5

"Morning, Clara," Tess said. "You're a sleepyhead today. I thought I'd have to wake you."

Clara wasn't a sleepyhead at all. She had been up for a while, getting ready for Special Friend Day. She wore the pretty pink dress that Mama had given her. She hoped Ashley's mother hadn't talked to the principal. Clara wondered what would happen if Mrs. Singh couldn't be her special friend. Maybe she'd have to wait in the library until the bell rang.

She poured a bowl of Apple Cinnamon Cheerios and, when Tess wasn't watching, picked them up with her fingers to eat them. Calvin was playing hockey with his cereal and spoon. Daddy was reading the *Toronto Star* sports section.

Tess glanced at the clock. "Better get moving. Don't forget, you have to get to school early today." She sighed and said, "Clara, please use your spoon." Clara didn't know why they tasted better when she ate them with her fingers, but they did.

Splat! Calvin knocked his glass over, and orange juice went everywhere. All over Calvin's pyjamas. All over Daddy's newspaper.

All over Clara's pink dress.

"I hate you!" she shouted. "I wish you were never born!"

Clara ran to her bedroom and slammed the door. She ripped the dress over her head and tossed it in the pile with yesterday's jeans. She pulled her robe out of the same pile and yanked it on.

"I hate you!" she shouted again, in case anyone missed it the first time. "Stupid Calvin," she said. She threw a couple of books on the floor. "Stupid brat."

She heard a knock. "Clara," Tess called, "are you okay?"

"No, I'm not okay!"

"Calvin's sorry about the orange juice."

"I don't care!"

Tess opened the door a crack. "I know you wanted to wear your dress. But there's nothing we can do. I'll wash it today and you can wear it to school tomorrow."

"But today is Special Friend Day. Why can't Calvin ever be good?"

"He didn't do it on purpose, hon. What else can you wear?"

"Nothing." Clara burst into tears.

Tess slipped through the door and hugged Clara. "Wouldn't you know it, today's laundry day, so most of your stuff's dirty. Let's see what's in your closet."

There wasn't much. Her sailor dress, which didn't really fit anymore, was hanging at the side. Clara was too old to wear a sailor dress. But the only other things in the closet were jeans and T-shirts. The other girls would be wearing dresses.

"Which would you like to wear?" Tess asked.

"I guess I'll wear the sailor dress." Calvin had

ruined everything.

"Finish your breakfast first and *then* get dressed," Tess said. "You'll have to scoot."

Clara pulled on her housecoat. She was hungry. The orange juice had landed in her bowl so she poured some cereal in a clean bowl. She poured some for Calvin, too, even though she still hated him. He could get his own spoon.

Daddy and Calvin came back in the kitchen. Calvin was in dry clothes, and he was carrying Poppy by the ear. Daddy said, "Calvin, I think you wanted to say something to Clara."

"Sorry," Calvin said, not sounding sorry at all.

"Keep your orange juice away from me," Clara said. "If you spill it again, I'll kill you."

"Please don't say that, Clara," Daddy said.

Clara fumed over her cereal. Why did Daddy only care about Calvin's feelings? It was her day that had been ruined, but Daddy had gone off to change Calvin's clothes, and left Tess to help Clara.

While she was getting dressed, Clara decided that if she couldn't wear the dress Mama bought,

50

she'd take something that belonged to her. She wished she could wear some of her perfume. Daddy kept Mama's perfume bottle on his dresser and sometimes he let Clara smell it. Every time she sniffed it, she closed her eyes and remembered Mama. But if she wore the perfume today, Daddy would smell it and know she'd been touching the bottle without his permission.

She peeked out the bathroom door. Daddy and Tess were in the kitchen with Calvin. Nobody paid any attention when she snuck around the corner into Daddy's bedroom. She knew where he kept Mama's scarves. She rooted through the drawer until she found the one Mama had worn last year on Valentine's Day. The scarf was red and pink, filled with gold swirls.

When she came out, Tess had Clara's coat in one hand and her backpack in the other. Clara wrapped Mama's scarf around the handle of the backpack. Daddy and Tess glanced at each other, but neither of them said anything about it. Daddy leaned over and kissed Clara's cheek. He always stayed with Calvin until Tess was back from taking Clara to school.

As Clara pulled on her coat, Tess said to Daddy, "She needs new clothes. That dress is too short, and she's growing out of almost everything."

"I didn't notice," Daddy said.

Clara jerked her head up. Tess was frowning, and Daddy was sitting at the table with his coffee cup stopped halfway to his mouth. Clara liked that Tess was standing up for her. And she liked that Daddy was in trouble. She was still cross at him.

"I'm sorry, sweetie," Daddy said to Clara. "We'll go shopping on the weekend, and buy you some clothes."

Usually they listened to Tess's hip-hop CDs in the car stereo on the way to school, but today Tess turned the music down.

"Don't forget that I'm picking you and Jenny up after school for dance class," Tess said.

"Miss Tabitha said we can't be late because she's measuring us for our costumes."

Tess paused. "You don't like ballet, do you?"

Clara was amazed. "How did you know?"

"I can tell. Ballet wasn't my thing, either." They were stopped at a traffic light, and Tess twisted around in the driver's seat to catch Clara's eye. "I'm a fan of people finishing what they start, but not when it makes them miserable. Why don't you talk about it with your dad?"

"I wish I could. But it's hard talking to him. Every time I mention Mama, Daddy gets so sad. And he loves watching me dance, just like Mama did."

A horn sounded from behind them. The light had turned green.

"Give him a chance, and he might surprise you," Tess said. "Your dad doesn't always know what to do, but he loves you a ton."

When they got to school, Clara waved good-bye to Tess and ran to her class. She was relieved to see Mrs. Singh waiting by the door, smiling at Clara. Maybe Jenny was right about Ashley.

"I'm glad you're here," Mrs. Singh said. "If you didn't come, I was afraid I'd have to take over from Mr. Hahn."

Clara peeked through the door. Mr. Hahn was standing beside a lemonade pitcher and a plate of cookies. Along the back wall was the pioneer unit display they'd done before Christmas. Clara had loved visiting Black Creek Pioneer Village, and her scrapbook was full of stories and pictures about pioneer life.

Most of the kids were already there. Stephanie and her mom were over by the pioneer display. She grinned and waved at Clara. Ashley and her mom stood next to Stephanie. Mrs. Mellor was beautiful in her fur coat.

Clara wondered what it would be like if Mrs. Mellor were her mother. She imagined spending a day with her. First, Mrs. Mellor would take Clara to a tennis store and buy her a tennis outfit. Then they'd go to a mall and buy Clara three hair bands — one pink, one red, and one pink and red. Clara would wear the tennis outfit and pink hair band, and she and Mrs. Mellor would go out for a chocolate milkshake.

She didn't really wish that Mrs. Mellor was her mother. Of course, then Ashley would be her sister. And Clara's daydream didn't include Ashley. Clara inched closer to Mrs. Singh.

"I enjoyed your family history," Mrs. Singh said, pointing to Clara's project on the wall. "How did you learn these interesting stories about your background?"

"My aunt Bridget came to see us at Christmas. She told us funny stories about everyone in the family." Clara had been astonished to hear that Mama once got a scolding for climbing on the roof.

"You can tell those stories to *your* children someday," Mrs. Singh said.

Clara had loved drawing the tree, and printing her parents' and grandparents' names in the branches. Her name was with Calvin's in the trunk.

Mrs. Singh smiled at Clara. "Your stories are wonderful, especially when you write about life with Calvin. Do you suppose your father used to be like Calvin when he was young?"

"No way!" Clara said. Daddy wouldn't have spilled orange juice on someone's favourite dress.

"Mrs. Singh," called Mr. Hahn. One of the middle school teachers was standing beside him.

Clara and Mrs. Singh went over to see what he wanted.

"I'm afraid I have to go," Mr. Hahn said. "We have a situation on the playground with a couple of grade eight boys. Sorry to leave you."

"We'll be fine," Mrs. Singh said. As he strode out the door, she turned to Clara. "I should stay close to the refreshments table, and I'd love it if you stayed close to me."

They talked about Clara's family tree for a minute, but then another few moms and kids came in and Mrs. Singh had to serve them.

Clara wandered over to the self-portraits the class had done last month from torn pieces of construction paper. Most of the kids looked happy in their portraits, but Clara noticed for the first time that she wasn't smiling.

The classroom was almost full. All the other kids were with their mothers. And now Clara was by herself.

Clara had never missed Mama more than she

did right now. And there was nothing she could invent to stop missing her.

"Nice dress." Ashley had wandered up beside her. "You wore it for the class picture in grade two." Mrs. Mellor was still chatting with Stephanie's mom by the pioneer display.

"No I didn't," Clara said. "This is a new one, exactly like the old one." She felt her face burning. Jenny and her mom were nearby, and Jenny looked at Clara with a puzzled expression.

"Right," Ashley said as she sauntered off.

"All done," Mrs. Singh said, joining Clara. "I've put up a sign telling people to help themselves. Tell me about your self-portrait. You did a beautiful job. The first time I saw it, I knew exactly whose it was."

When the bell rang, Mrs. Singh went to her desk and most of the mothers left the classroom. Jenny made a beeline for Clara.

"Why did you lie about your dress?" Jenny asked.

Clara's stomach felt as if it was full of wriggling snakes. "I don't know. I told you I say dumb things around Ashley."

"Don't tell lies. That always makes things worse."

"I won't lie anymore," Clara said.

Jenny went to sit at their table while Clara dawdled behind. Was Jenny mad at her?

This was the worst day ever. It was bad enough that Mama couldn't come. But now she had lied to Ashley, and Jenny had heard her. She didn't want Jenny to think she was a liar. What if Jenny thought she couldn't trust Clara anymore?

And now she had to wear her stupid sailor dress for the rest of the day, reminding her that she looked like a baby, and that sometimes she told lies.

6

Clara peeked one eye open a bit. The sun was shining in her bedroom window, but she didn't have to hurry. It was Saturday morning.

Saturday mornings were the best. She could lie in bed wiggling her toes, or wiggling nothing at all. She rolled over on her side and closed her eyes again. Today was a good day to wiggle nothing at all.

Her door opened gently and tiny footsteps padded across the floor. Someone poked her eyelid.

"Read to me," Calvin said.

How did Calvin know today was Saturday? Monday through Friday, Calvin went into

Daddy's room while Daddy got ready for work. But he knew when it was Saturday — maybe because Tess wasn't there — and he wanted to see Clara.

She opened her eyes and checked the clock. 7:33. Not bad, for Calvin. He shoved *Puddleman* at her. "Read to me," he repeated.

"Please?" Clara coaxed.

"Please," Calvin said, jamming the book in her lap.

Clara opened it up. She didn't mind reading to Calvin. Even though she was too old for his books, it was fun to read them again. "'One morning, Michael filled his sandbox with water and jumped in'."

Calvin was good for about half the book, but then he started trying to flip the pages ahead of Clara. When Clara said, "I can't read that fast," Calvin jumped off the bed.

"I'm hungry!" he said.

She stepped into her slippers and said, "Let's get breakfast."

They went out to the kitchen. Clara poured

him a bowl of cereal with no milk. "You are *not* drinking orange juice today," she said.

Calvin took his bowl in one hand and Poppy in the other, and went into the living room. Every Saturday he sat on the couch and stared at the blank TV screen until Clara turned it on. What would happen if one day she didn't? Would he stare at the blank screen all morning?

But she did turn it on, after she had poured herself some cereal, too. "Arthur" was beginning, her favourite cartoon.

Calvin had spilled Cheerios all over the couch. Good thing he didn't like milk on his cereal. Clara would have had a big mess to clean up. Sometimes she got tired of watching him.

When Mama was alive, she woke up early on Saturdays and made breakfast for everyone. Clara missed her pancakes and maple syrup, and she missed seeing Mama in her pyjamas on Saturday mornings. Daddy didn't make breakfast on Saturdays, and he wasn't even here to help clean up Calvin's spilled Cheerios.

At the end of the third cartoon, Clara stacked

their breakfast dishes in the dishwasher. She heard Daddy moving around in his bedroom. Calvin did too, because he ran down the hall and into Daddy's room.

"Come on in, guys," Daddy called. His hair was standing up and his chin was stubbly. It tickled Clara's face when he kissed her.

Clara loved Daddy's bedroom. Whenever she brought art home from school Daddy hung it somewhere in the house, and a lot of it ended up in here. The valentine she'd painted for him was on the wall next to Calvin's stick man.

Daddy also had the biggest bed in the house. He didn't let her jump on the bed, so she sat on the edge and bounced. She bounced until he said, "That's enough."

He chased Calvin over to the bed, and the three of them lay down together. "What are we going to do today?" Clara asked.

"I hear you're growing out of your clothes," he said. "Let's go shopping this morning before I get in more trouble with Tess." He winked. "What should we buy?"

Clara remembered how pretty Mrs. Mellor was. "A tennis outfit," she suggested.

"You don't play tennis. Let's keep it simple. Dresses or jeans?"

She thought for a minute, then said, "Jeans." Stephanie wore jeans and a hoodie most days and she looked great. "Jeans and hoodies."

"Sounds good," Daddy said. "At least your ballet costume will fit. If Miss Tabitha had measured you a month ago, it might be too small."

Clara bared her teeth and rolled her eyes up to make them go all white.

Daddy laughed. "What's up with the face?"

"Miss Tabitha. She yells at some of the kids when they don't get the steps the first time."

"I'm sure you're one of her star students. I can't wait to see your dance recital in May."

Clara bit her lip. This would be the perfect time to talk to Daddy.

Daddy went on. "The recital was Mama's favourite time of the year. It meant a lot to her that you loved to dance. When I see you on the stage, you remind me so much of her."

Clara sank back into the bed. She could *never* tell Daddy.

Suddenly music blared, and Daddy whirled to find Calvin pushing buttons on the clock radio.

"Whoa! That's too loud," Daddy said, lifting Calvin with one hand and switching off the radio with the other. "Tell you what. Why don't you guys go back to your cartoons while I get dressed? Then we'll leave for the mall."

On her way out of his bedroom, Clara stopped beside the dresser for a minute. The scarf was sitting where she'd left it after Special Friend Day, and next to it was Mama's glass perfume bottle.

Whenever Mama had bought perfume, she'd poured it in the bottle. Mama's grandmother had bought the bottle when she was young. She gave it to Mama's mother when she grew up, who gave it to Mama when she married Daddy.

"It always goes to the oldest daughter," Mama had said. "Someday I'll give it to you."

Clara wished she could have it now. The bottle was beautiful. But more than anything, she loved to smell the perfume that was inside. Daddy said that Mama's perfume smelled like roses. But Clara thought it smelled like a hug.

"Come on, daydreamer," Daddy said. "The sooner we get ready, the sooner you get new clothes."

* * *

When they got to the mall, Daddy stood in front of the map that showed all the stores. "I don't know where to shop," he said.

Clara wasn't sure either. But she knew where some of the girls bought their clothes. "How about Billie Jean's?"

They went to Billie Jean's, but Daddy frowned after he checked a couple of price tags. "These clothes are too expensive," he said, in a loud voice. "Let's try somewhere else."

Clara's face burned. She hoped no one had heard him.

They walked out. "How about Little Tykes?" Daddy said.

They gazed in the store window. One mannequin was wearing a long white dress, like a wedding gown for kids. The other one wore a sailor dress.

"Those are pretty," he said. "Should we go in?"

"This is a store for little kids," Clara said. The last thing she needed was another sailor dress. "Let's go to Armstrong's." That's where Mama had bought Clara's pink dress.

When they reached Armstrong's, Daddy said, "These prices are better." Clara wandered down the aisles, gathering clothes to try on. For once, Calvin was happy in his stroller, ramming his dump truck into the side of the tray.

Daddy caught up to her, with some clothes in his arms. "I found a few things you might try on," he said.

Clara looked at them in shock. A blue striped T-shirt, a red sweatshirt with a basketball player … "Those are boys' clothes, Daddy," she hissed. Thank goodness none of the kids from school were around.

"How can you tell?" Daddy asked, bewildered.

"I just know. The girls' clothes are on this side of the store."

She kept browsing while Daddy hung up the boys' shirts. But he was back in a minute with a new armful of clothes. "These are definitely girls' clothes because I found them on this side of the store." He smiled proudly as he held them up.

Clara peeked at one of the tags and laughed. "These jeans are size 6. I wore size 6 in kindergarten!"

Daddy set his pile down. "I'll let you pick out your own things. You know what you need better than I do."

As Clara took another pair of jeans off the rack, he asked, "How was Special Friend Day?"

"Good," Clara said. She hesitated. "Were you sad that I took Mrs. Singh?"

"No. She was a great choice."

"But I didn't take you." Clara pulled a blue hoodie off the shelf and added it to her pile.

"Clara, you worry about so many things." Daddy took the pile of clothes out of her arms. "If you ever want to talk — I don't always know what to say, but I can listen."

I know you can listen, she thought. *I just don't*

want to make you sad, and that happens when I talk about Mama.

But now she felt the words slipping out. "I liked going with Mrs. Singh but I wish I could have taken Mama." She looked up at Daddy. "I miss Mama."

"I miss her too," he whispered, giving her a big hug.

"Can I help you?" the salesgirl asked, staring at the pile of clothes caught in the middle of their hug.

"Go ahead, Clara. You'll be fine," Daddy said.

On her way to the changing rooms, Clara saw a display of hair bands on the counter. She chose a pink one and handed it to Daddy. Maybe if she had the right clothes and a pink hair band, things would get better.

7

Nobody could concentrate the day before March Break. After lunch, Mrs. Singh didn't even try to teach. Kerry's mom brought in chocolate chip cookies and fruit punch, and they had a class party.

Clara munched on a cookie and listened to the kids talk about March Break. Daddy was taking Calvin and her to a maple syrup farm on Sunday afternoon. They went there every year and she loved it. The best part was when the farmer poured boiling syrup on the snow to make candy.

Daddy had to work during March Break week, but Tess promised to take them skating. If the snow lasted, they'd go tobogganing too.

"We're going to Club Med tomorrow," Ashley said. "We go to the same resort every year and stay in a deluxe room. Mom plays tennis, Daddy golfs, and Mallory and I go to circus camp. I can't wait to try the trapeze."

"You're lucky," Stephanie said. "We're going to the ski chalet again. Mom says if we have a chalet, we should use it while the snow's good. Where are *you* going, Jenny?"

"Visiting Grandma and Grandpa in Florida. We're going to Disney World!"

"How 'bout you, Clara?" Stephanie asked.

"She never goes anywhere," Ashley said and took a sip from her juice box.

Clara's face went red. "For your information, I *am* going away!"

"Where are you going?" Stephanie asked.

"Mexico," Clara blurted.

"You are not," Ashley said.

"Yes I am! We're staying in a deluxe room too, and we'll go swimming every day."

Ashley rolled her eyes.

"She wouldn't say she was going to Mexico if

she wasn't," Jenny said.

Clara got that wriggling-snake feeling in her stomach again. Mexico? Why had she said that? Maybe everyone would forget.

"So, will you send me a postcard from Mexico?" Ashley asked. She said the word "Mexico" like it was dripping with slime.

Clara shrugged. "I might be too busy. Will you send me a postcard from Med Club?"

"Not likely. And it's Club Med. Don't you know anything?"

Clara didn't say anything. It was better if she kept her mouth shut around Ashley. She should have kept her mouth shut a minute ago.

"Let's compare our suntans when we get back." Ashley said. "The one with the worst tan is the loser."

Mrs. Singh stood up at the front of the class. "Boys and girls," she said, "when you're done with your drinks and plates, please put them in the recycling box."

Clara carried hers to the back of the room. She didn't even want to finish her cookie. She had

71

a terrible feeling that she was going to be the loser.

Jenny was at the back of the room, too. Clara pulled her aside and whispered, "I'm in trouble."

"Why?"

"We're not going to Mexico."

"Why did you say you were?"

"I don't know. I told you I say dumb things when I'm around Ashley. She just made me mad."

Jenny folded her arms. "I stood up for you. I told them you were telling the truth. I can't believe you lied again."

"I didn't mean to."

"You promised me you wouldn't lie anymore," Jenny said. Then she went and sat down at Lexy's table.

Was Jenny cross at her? Clara couldn't move. Now she had lied twice to Jenny, even though she'd only meant to lie to Ashley. Did that mean Jenny wouldn't be her friend?

She was about to go over to talk with Jenny when Mrs. Singh called her. "Clara, can I see you for a minute?"

Clara went cold. Had Mrs. Singh heard what she said? Did she know Clara was making up the story about Mexico?

But Mrs. Singh wasn't angry at all. "You did such a beautiful job sharpening my pencils the other day. Would you mind sharpening my pencil crayons before you go?"

The bell rang, and Jenny raced out with the others. Clara tried to do a good job with the pencil crayons, but she was hurrying and she kept breaking the red one. By the time she finished, Jenny's locker was closed and there was no sign of her.

Clara knew there was only one thing to do. She had to turn the lie into the truth.

Clara had to talk Daddy into taking her to Mexico.

*   *   *

The hay wagon jiggled down the hill. The ride was tippy, and Clara's stomach felt tippy too. She grabbed Daddy's arm and held tight. Calvin was trying to get away from Daddy. When Daddy wasn't watching, he picked up a handful of hay

73

and tossed it on the other people in the wagon.

When the wagon stopped, everyone climbed off. "Thanks for the tour," Daddy said to the driver. Clara clutched a bottle of maple syrup against her parka as she climbed down.

"You're quiet today," Daddy said as they walked back to the parking lot. "Everything alright?"

"I wish we had more time together."

"Me too. I'd like to be with you guys all the time."

"Hey," Clara said, as if she'd just thought of it, "You should take next week off work."

"It isn't that easy to get time off. Besides, Tess has a great week planned for you. What would we do if I was on holidays?"

"I don't know," Clara said. "We might go away together. Hey, we could go to Mexico! Wouldn't that be great?"

Daddy laughed. "That would be great. But going to Mexico costs a lot of pesos. And I'm too busy at work to take holidays. Why don't you have a pretend beach party this week?"

That wouldn't do at all. But Clara didn't say anything else until they had pulled out of the parking lot.

"I hear you can get a trip for a lot less money if you go at the last minute. Let's check it out!"

Daddy looked at Clara in the rear-view mirror. "We're not going to Mexico."

Clara bit her lip. This was her last chance. "It's just that — well, I *have* to go to Mexico for my school project. Mrs. Singh said we had to pick a country and go there for March Break. If I don't go, I might fail!"

Daddy pulled the car over to the side of the road. "What's going on, Clara?"

"I told you. Mrs. Singh said we had to go to a country —"

He looked cross. Time for the truth.

"Everyone else in my class is going on a trip next week. Ashley's going to Med Club, Jenny's going to Florida — everyone's going somewhere. I didn't want to be the only one staying home, so I said I was going on a trip, too."

"To Mexico," Daddy said.

Maybe he understood after all!

Daddy sighed. "You told the kids you were going to Mexico. Now you want to go there so they won't know you were lying."

Clara looked at her fingernails. "Jenny already knows, and she's mad at me."

"I'm sorry about that. She's a good friend. But sometimes we make mistakes and we have to learn from them. I think you're going to learn something from this mistake."

"Daddy, I promise I'll learn something! I've learned something already. I won't tell another lie."

"Good."

"But can we please go to Mexico?"

"No."

Clara sat back in her seat and blinked away a tear. "It's no fair. They were bragging, and Ashley said I never go anywhere. I'm tired of being the only kid who's different."

"Don't worry about what Ashley thinks. We can't possibly compete with her family. And I don't want to compete with them. I don't want to be like Mr. Mellor. Do you want to be like Ashley?"

Did she want to be like Ashley? She wouldn't want to be mean. But Ashley went on fun trips and had a million toys and got to do everything she wanted.

Clara wanted to be a bit like Ashley.

"Maybe the others were bragging. Maybe Ashley said some things that were unkind," Daddy said. "But you told a lie, and that's never right."

He pulled back on the road.

Clara felt awful. She hadn't really expected Daddy to take them to Mexico, but she'd hoped he might. Now everyone would know she was a liar. She tried not to cry, but first one tear fell, then another, and another. She didn't want Daddy to see that she was crying, but her nose started to run. If she didn't sniffle, it would run into her mouth. She sniffled.

"Oh, Clara," Daddy said. "Just a minute ... Where are those tissues? ... We have tissues in here somewhere."

He pulled over again. He checked the glove compartment. He rooted around under the front seat. He dragged out Calvin's diaper bag and handed her a diaper wipe. Clara hadn't blown her nose into a diaper wipe before, but it was better than her parka sleeve. She blew.

Clara wished she could invent a car with wings that could fly to Mexico. They would go this afternoon, and they'd stay in a hotel with a deluxe room. They could fly back to Toronto tomorrow night, so Daddy wouldn't have to miss work.

She blew her nose again. "What if Jenny doesn't want to be my friend anymore?"

"Tell her you're sorry, and mean it. Promise not to tell any more lies, and follow through. It's worth it, to have a friend like Jenny."

Clara knew that what he said was true. She just wished she didn't have to wait a whole week to see Jenny again.

*   *   *

When Tess came in on Monday morning, she hugged Clara. "Your dad told me what happened

78

with Jenny. That's pretty rough."

Clara nodded. "Daddy said I should tell her I'm sorry, and never lie again," she said, not catching Tess's eye.

"Sounds like a good plan."

"Do you think I should buy her a present?" Buying a present would be easier than apologizing.

"No. She'll be cool if you say you're sorry."

"Usually it's easy talking to Jenny." Clara sighed. "Easier than talking to Daddy."

"I guess you haven't asked him about ballet yet."

"I wanted to. But then he said that he loved watching me dance, like Mama did. I couldn't tell him then."

"It's okay to feel sad. Of course you both miss her — she was wonderful. I think your daddy would love to talk about her. He thinks about her a lot, just like you do."

Just then, Calvin ran into the kitchen.

"Okay, guys, eat your breakfast, because we have a jam-packed day," Tess said. "We'll start at the toboggan hill. When you get good and cold, we'll come home for my world-famous hot chocolate. After Calvin's nap, we'll go skating."

Clara was surprised at how much fun she had that week. Tess took them to the CN Tower, and Clara loved trying to look for their house from the observation deck. She went skating every day, once at the outdoor rink at Harbourfront, and she practiced skating backward until she was almost perfect. She borrowed *Ramona and Her Father* from the library, and laughed when Picky-Picky ate the pumpkin. Best of all, ballet had been cancelled for March Break.

Every time she thought about Jenny, she tried to decide what to say to her. It would be hard, but she'd do anything to be Jenny's friend again. Was Jenny thinking about her while she was in Florida?

They were at the skating rink Friday afternoon when Clara saw Stephanie. Clara thought about hiding. Too late — Stephanie saw her and glided over.

"Hi, Clara. Wanna skate with me?"

"Sure."

They skated around the rink a couple of times. Then Clara said, "Weren't you skiing this week?"

"We were," Stephanie said, "but Dad had to come back early for work." She swivelled so she was skating backward, facing Clara.

Clara was thinking hard. She could say her dad had to come back early, too. But she was tired of lying.

"You know when I said we were going to Mexico?"

"Yeah?"

"We didn't go anywhere. I made it up."

"I thought so," Stephanie said.

"How did you know?"

"Ashley's always right. If she said you're not going to Mexico, then you're not going to Mexico." Stephanie spun around, skating by Clara's side again.

"You're not mad at me?" Clara asked.

Stephanie shrugged. "You didn't have to lie. Lots of kids stayed in Toronto this week, and they didn't say they were going to Mexico. But I'm not mad at you."

Clara felt better than she had all week. She'd told the truth, and Stephanie wasn't mad at her. "Let's get some hot chocolate," Clara said. "Last one there is a dirty rotten egg!"

It was great that Stephanie didn't mind that Clara had told a lie.

But would Jenny forgive her?

8

On Monday morning, Tess sent Clara with extra cookies in her lunch. "You can share these with Jenny," she said. "A peace offering. But you still have to apologize." Clara knew that, but sharing the cookies would make it easier.

Tess had put four chocolate chip cookies in a little Rubbermaid tub. "Two for you and two for Jenny." If it had been Mama, she would've baked sugar cookies. But chocolate chip cookies were good, too.

When she got to school, Clara checked out the classroom. Most of the kids didn't have tans. Jenny and Ashley hadn't arrived yet.

If only Jenny would hurry up and get there.

Clara had practiced what she'd say, and she was bursting to get it over with.

Mrs. Singh shushed everyone. "Girls and boys, I know you're excited about your week off, but please be quiet while I take attendance. We'll have a chance to talk about our holidays in a few minutes. Kerry?"

"Here."

And then Ashley walked in. Everyone in the class turned and stared.

Ashley had a terrible frown, and she had a cast on her left arm. And she had no suntan. She slammed her books on the table.

"Please join us quietly, Ashley. I'm taking attendance," Mrs. Singh said.

"*Here*," Ashley said, glaring. Clara peeked over at Stephanie, but Stephanie shrugged her shoulders. She didn't know what was wrong, either.

Jenny didn't come to school. Was she sick? Was she so mad at Clara that she'd switched schools?

The kids at every table were drawing a bar

graph. Usually Clara loved taking surveys and filling out the graphs, but when the morning recess bell rang, she was wiggling around in her chair from trying to pay attention. As she pulled on her coat and boots, she decided she'd call Jenny the minute she got home tonight. Even if she was going to another school, Clara had to tell her she was sorry.

While Clara was playing freeze tag at recess with the others, Stephanie ran out to join them.

"Can I play with you guys?" she asked. "Ashley has to stay inside for recess."

"What happened to her?" Clara asked.

"She broke her arm on the trapeze the first day at circus camp, and couldn't go back. It rained the whole time so nobody got a tan. She said her parents fought all week and she had the worst trip ever."

Clara tried to feel sorry for Ashley. It would be sad to have a holiday like that. But part of her was happy that Ashley had had a terrible time. She was sorry about her broken arm, but she was glad Ashley didn't have a tan.

"You can play with us," Clara said shyly. "We're playing freeze tag."

"I'll be It!" Stephanie said, and the other girls screamed and ran.

* * *

After recess, it was reading time. Clara was starting a new *Ramona* book when she felt a poke in the arm. Ashley was jabbing her with her pencil.

"Ow!" Clara whispered. "Are you trying to break *my* arm, too?"

"I'm going to tell everyone about you," Ashley said. "You didn't go to Mexico. You didn't go anywhere last week."

Clara's stomach twisted but she tried to act calm. "Everyone knows that. I went skating with Stephanie."

"You did not!" Ashley said.

"Girls, you should be reading, not talking," Mrs. Singh said.

"You did not," Ashley repeated, when Mrs. Singh looked away. "She was skiing. You're lying again."

"If you don't believe me, ask Stephanie,"

Clara said.

Ashley checked to make sure Mrs. Singh wasn't watching, then leaned over toward Stephanie. Clara tried to hear what they said, but she only heard whispers until Ashley said, "Why would you go skating with her?"

"I'm moving you to another table, Ashley," Mrs. Singh said. "Please sit between Lexy and Jackson."

Ashley pushed away from the table, picking up her books with her right arm. "My mom's gonna talk to the principal about you," she hissed at Clara. "This is your fault."

Clara remembered what Jenny had said about Ashley's threats to go to the principal. She didn't worry too much, and it was better without Ashley sitting at her table.

Clara picked up her bag at lunchtime and headed to the lunchroom with the other girls. While she ate her sandwich, she listened to Ashley complain about her trip. Clara wanted to mention the worst-tan contest, but decided to leave it alone.

"Who likes Miss Tabitha?" Stephanie asked. A couple of the girls giggled.

Clara made a face. "She's so grumpy. Every week she gets mad at me about something."

Ashley shrugged. "She never gets mad at me. But I know our dance routine. If you learned it, and if she didn't have to tell you every week to point your toes, maybe she'd stop being mad at you."

Nobody else said anything. No one wanted to disagree with Ashley.

Finally Stephanie spoke up. "I don't like the barre exercises, but I like everything else." Clara knew that Stephanie was trying to make everyone happy.

She realized that she had no one to share her cookies with since Jenny wasn't there. But Stephanie was sitting to her left. Stephanie had skated with Clara, and had played tag with her at morning recess. Clara wanted to share with her.

"Would you like a chocolate chip cookie?" Clara asked. "Tess made them."

Stephanie was about to reach for one. "Don't

eat those," Ashley said. "Clara's nanny made them. They're probably full of cooties."

Stephanie hesitated. "I've had Tess's cookies before, and they're good. Besides, I don't think there's such a thing as cooties."

"If you eat one of those cookies, you'll get sick. And then I won't come to your house after school."

Stephanie drew her hand back. "Not today," she said to Clara. "Thanks anyhow."

Clara finished her first cookie. She didn't want to eat the second one, let alone the third and fourth. She couldn't believe what Ashley had said. Tess was the second-best cookie baker ever, after Mama.

She was still steaming when she went to her locker. On the way, she noticed Mrs. Singh hanging up the bar graphs they'd been working on. She rapped on the door and Mrs. Singh turned around.

"Hello, Clara," she said. "Did you and Calvin have a fun March Break?"

"We did." Clara thought for a minute. "Tess

took us to some fun places. One day we had lunch at the Old Spaghetti Factory, and then went skating at Harbourfront. Tess bought us hot chocolate, and Calvin spilt it all over his snowpants."

Mrs. Singh laughed. "Calvin's a rascal, isn't he?"

Clara thought "rascal" was a polite way of saying it, but she nodded. "Tess didn't get mad at him. She just said we'd throw his pants in the wash when we got home."

Mrs. Singh set down her masking tape and leaned on the edge of her desk. "Tess really cares for you and Calvin."

"Yeah," Clara said. She pulled the Rubbermaid container out of her lunch box. "She packed some extra cookies today. Would you like one?"

Mrs. Singh chose a cookie. "That's generous of you to share."

Clara felt good enough to eat her second cookie with Ms. Singh.

*   *   *

That afternoon, Clara actually had fun, now that Ashley was at the other table. She and Stephanie worked together to make a plaster fossil of a maple leaf. But at the end of the day, right before the bell rang, Clara saw Mrs. Mellor waiting outside the classroom.

Mrs. Mellor came in the classroom as the kids were leaving. She wore her fur coat over black yoga pants. She was smiling like Ashley sometimes did, the smile that was glued on a mad face.

Clara wondered if Mrs. Mellor had decided to complain about Mrs. Singh being Clara's Special Friend. She slowly packed up her books, listening to the conversation.

"Thank you for coming in," Mrs. Singh started.

"If Ashley is having issues with the other students, I'm sure it's because of her broken arm. It was a real disappointment for her."

"Perhaps we should wait until we have some privacy," Mrs. Singh said, nodding at Clara. Clara picked up her books and scurried out of the room.

91

Ashley in trouble? Clara thought Ashley made up all the rules, even for the teachers.

She ran out to meet Calvin and Tess. Calvin ran around Tess and Clara in a big circle.

"How was Jenny?" Tess asked.

"She wasn't here today," Clara said. "I'll call her when we get home. Maybe she's sick."

"That's too bad. Did you find someone else to share the cookies with?"

"I gave one to Mrs. Singh. Calvin can eat the last one." Clara paused. "Tess, you make great cookies. Anyone who doesn't like your cookies probably doesn't like good food."

Tess reached out and hugged Clara. "Thanks, hon. Your mom made the best cookies ever. But I'm glad you like mine too."

Clara nodded.

"Your mom kept her recipes in a binder," Tess said. "Anytime you want to try one, let's work on it together. I think you have her magic touch in the kitchen."

"Really?" breathed Clara. She'd never thought about being like Mama.

"You're a natural. How about the Rice Krispie Squares you helped me make during March Break? They were awesome!"

Clara remembered the Rice Krispie Squares. *They really were awesome*, she thought. They hadn't had quite enough Rice Krispies, so the squares were extra gooey. Clara and Calvin had loved them so much that Tess had said she'd make them that way every time.

When they got home, Clara was thinking about how mean Ashley was. Then she thought about the kind people in her life. Mrs. Singh, who always had time to listen. Tess, who looked after them, and who had loved Mama, too. And Jenny.

Jenny was a true friend. She wasn't mean to her, or to anyone else. They had fun when they played tag at school, and when they built snowmen at Clara's house.

Clara still had to make it up to her. Did Jenny want to be friends?

Clara picked up the phone when they got inside. Her apology wasn't going to wait until tomorrow morning. She took the phone to her room and called Jenny's number. While she waited for someone to pick up, she sat on the edge of her bed and swung her legs. The phone rang seven times. No answer.

Where was Jenny?

9

Daddy was in his bedroom trying to find socks to wear to church. "Clara, are these two blacks, or a black and a brown?" He was terrible with colours.

"They're brown and blue," Clara said.

"Can you help me find black ones?"

Clara went to the clean laundry pile and sorted. Calvin picked up a grey sock and dangled it over his nose. "I'm an elephant!" he said, and made a trumpeting sound.

Daddy laughed. "You're the tiniest elephant I've ever seen. Can I have a ride?"

Calvin giggled as Daddy pretended to get on his back.

March Break had been over a week ago and

still Jenny wasn't back. Clara was starting to think she really had changed schools. She'd called three times last week and nobody was answering. Clara sat with the other girls at lunch every day, but it wasn't the same as sitting with Jenny. Ballet without Jenny had been awful, too — Miss Tabitha had been cross at Clara, and the madder she got, the more mistakes Clara made. If Jenny had been there, she would have cheered Clara up.

Clara wished she could invent a magic wand that would make Miss Tabitha nice. But she didn't think even an inventor could be that powerful.

Clara should have been happy that the theme of the recital was *The Lion King*, because it was one of her favourite movies. But her class was dancing to the song "Be Prepared." Clara hated when Scar sang that song in the movie, and she hated dancing to it every week in class. The only good thing about the recital was the costume. The girls wore little beige skirts that twirled when they spun around. Clara didn't like ballet, but she loved spinning in that skirt.

"Here, Daddy." Clara tossed a pair of socks on

his bed and walked over to the dresser.

The top of his dresser was a jumble. Clara saw two other pairs of black socks that he might have worn. She also saw a sports magazine, a handful of change, two pens, and a family picture from when Calvin was a baby.

Clara reached over everything to the back of the dresser and lifted Mama's bottle of perfume.

Daddy came over. "You can look, but don't touch." He reached for the bottle.

"Can I smell it?" Clara asked.

Daddy held the bottle in his hands. Gently, as if he was afraid it might break. He lifted the stopper, and immediately Clara smelled Mama. She leaned over to take in the scent.

"Joy," Daddy said. "Mama's perfume was called 'Joy'." He sat quietly for a minute.

"I wanna smell," Calvin shouted, lumbering over, still holding the sock on his nose.

He took a quick sniff, then Daddy replaced the stopper on the bottle. "We'll be late for church if I don't get those socks on. Calvin, can I wear yours?"

"No!" Calvin said, bending down to grab his feet. "*My* socks!"

"Thanks for your help, Clara," Daddy said. "We should go."

They walked out, and Daddy shut the bedroom door behind them. Clara slouched after him, kicking at the floor as she went. He acted as if he didn't trust her to be careful with Mama's things.

They were going to church now, but later she'd go back into Daddy's room. Without Daddy.

* * *

Every Sunday, they had grilled cheese sandwiches for lunch. Daddy said it was a tradition. Clara knew it was all that Daddy could cook. Except for Shake and Bake, which they'd have for dinner.

On Friday after school, Tess had stayed late to bake sugar cookies with Clara. Clara was surprised how good they were, and she and Tess had hidden the container so Daddy and Calvin wouldn't eat them all at once. Clara brought out the last of them for dessert.

After lunch, Clara cleared the dishes and helped load the dishwasher. Plates facing in, knives with sharp points down.

The phone rang, and Daddy picked it up.

"I do it," Calvin said, crowding Clara at the dishwasher.

"Not the knives," Clara said, trying to swat him away. Calvin shoved her, hard.

"That would. be super," Daddy said as he waved his arm for them to be quiet. "I'll mark it on the calendar. Does she want to talk to Clara?"

Clara shoved Calvin back. He started to cry.

"Leave your brother alone," Daddy said, holding his hand over the phone.

Why did he blame her for everything?

He handed the phone over. "Jenny wants to talk to you," he said.

Clara took the phone from Daddy. She wondered if Jenny was calling from Florida, or from her new school. "Hi!" she said. She bit her lip. Was Jenny calling to say she didn't want to be her friend?

"Hi!" Jenny said. "We're back!"

Clara's hand felt sweaty on the phone. "Where have you been?"

"When we got to Florida, Mom and Dad told us we were staying for two weeks. What a great surprise! We went to Disney World twice, and Ryan was afraid of Mickey Mouse." She laughed. "And we went swimming every day." She paused. "How about you?"

"We didn't go anywhere. I missed you." She took a deep breath. "The whole time you were gone, I was worried that we weren't friends anymore."

"Why?"

"Because I lied to Ashley about Mexico."

"I always want to be your friend."

"I always want to be your friend, too." Clara's heart was a balloon, getting bigger and bigger. "I'm sorry I lied. I thought about what I said, and I've decided I'm only going to tell the truth from now on."

"That's great!" Jenny had a smile in her voice.

"And I'll try to ignore what Ashley says. Especially when she's mean."

"If you need any help, I promise to back you up." Jenny paused a minute. "Oh, did your dad tell you why we called? Mom was asking him about my birthday party. I wanted to check if you could come before we sent out the invitations."

"Really?"

"Yeah!" Jenny said. "I wouldn't have a birthday party without my best friend!"

Jenny said she was her best friend! Clara felt warm all over. "I can't wait!"

"I told my mom how great Tess's chocolate cake is. So she's going to ask Tess for the recipe. Is that okay with you?"

"Sure," Clara said. Tess *did* make great chocolate cake. And someday Clara would make chocolate cake that was as good as Mama's and Tess's. "You're my best friend, and you should have the best cake!"

"Anyway, I have to go and do the invitations, but I'll see you tomorrow."

When Clara hung up the phone, Daddy said, "Time for golf." He swung Calvin onto his shoulders and carried him into the living room. Clara turned on the dishwasher and followed them in.

"If I happen to doze off, would you keep an eye on Calvin?"

"Okay," Clara said. "But if he cries, don't blame me."

"No fighting, guys." Daddy lay down on the couch, and before the ads were over, his eyes were shut. He fell asleep every week watching golf, except in football season, when he fell asleep watching football.

Clara found the building blocks for Calvin, the big wooden set that she had loved when she was little.

"Play with me?" Calvin asked.

"Okay," Clara said. She helped him stack a few blocks to make a garage wall for his cars. This was when Clara loved Calvin the most — when he wasn't getting into trouble or spilling things.

Everyone said Calvin looked exactly like Daddy, and Clara never understood that. But when Calvin was busy with his cars or the blocks, sometimes he tucked his thumb between his fingers, like Daddy did. He was doing that now, with his left thumb tucked between his first two fingers. Clara wondered if that's why Daddy loved Calvin best.

Calvin started in on the second wall. He was concentrating on the garage and didn't notice when Clara slowly backed away from the blocks. Calvin was on his own. She had something more important to do.

Five minutes. That's all she needed. She'd be back before he noticed she was gone.

Clara crept down the hall, being careful to miss the creaky spot outside the kitchen. She opened Daddy's bedroom door, and tiptoed across to the dresser.

That beautiful perfume bottle! She just wanted to touch it for a minute. The bottle was beautifully carved and fragile, and the stopper was covered with roses. Clara could have held it in one hand. But she was being extra careful, so she used both hands.

Mama hadn't worn perfume every day. Only to church, and when she and Daddy went out at night. Clara remembered one time when Mama wore her long black dress, before she got sick. Clara hadn't wanted to let her go out that night. She'd wanted to touch Mama's velvet dress and her smooth pearls, and to smell her wonderful perfume.

And now Clara wanted to smell the perfume again. One tiny sniff, then she'd go back to play with Calvin. She slowly pulled the stopper out and —

Thud!

"Wah!"

It was Calvin.

"Waaah!"

Clara quickly set the bottle back on the dresser and ran to the kitchen. Daddy was already there and Calvin was screaming. And bleeding.

"Where are the paper towels? I need a paper towel! Oh, Clara, get me a facecloth!" Daddy had his hand under Calvin's chin. Calvin was screaming a lot. He was on the floor where he'd fallen and dragged the box of Apple Cinnamon Cheerios with him. Cheerios had spilled from the open box all over the place.

Clara ran into the bathroom and came back with a facecloth.

She knew it was her fault. She should have been watching him. She blinked to stop the tears from pouring down her face.

Daddy held the towel up to Calvin's mouth. Calvin was bleeding onto his shirt. Clara knew she should help Daddy wipe the blood up, but she couldn't move. He would probably be fine, but what if he wasn't? What if he went to the hospital, and never came back?

"You were supposed to be watching him. How did he get up on the counter?"

Clara said nothing. She pulled the dustpan out from under the sink, and swept up some of the crushed cereal. Calvin hadn't stopped crying, but at least he wasn't screaming anymore. Daddy held the towel against Calvin's lip and that stopped the bleeding, or at least slowed it down.

Clara was working very hard, and trying not to catch Daddy's eye. If she took a long time to clean up, maybe he'd forget to ask why she hadn't been in the room.

"Clara." Daddy hadn't forgotten. Calvin was sitting on one of his knees, sniffling. "I know I shouldn't have asked you to watch Calvin. Sometimes I ask you to do too much. But I wish you'd told me you were leaving the room. What happened? Where were you when your brother was being a mountain goat?"

"Um, I was in the other room."

"Yes?"

Clara paused. It would have been easy to say she'd been in the bathroom. But she'd promised Jenny she would tell the truth and she was going to keep that promise. "Smelling Mama's perfume," she said.

"I asked you not to do that without me there."

"Sorry, Daddy." But she was too worried about Calvin to think about anything else. "Is he going to be okay?"

Calvin wiggled, and Daddy examined his face. "No loose teeth, just a cut on his lip. He'll look like a boxer for a few days but he'll be fine."

Calvin beamed. Clara thought Calvin might enjoy looking like a boxer.

"He's not going to die?"

Daddy's face went soft. "Oh, Clara. He's not going to die." He patted his other knee. "Come here," he said. Clara sat down and hugged him hard. She needed to hold him, to feel the soft cotton of his shirt. Her arms didn't quite reach around him, but she held him as tightly as she could.

Daddy hugged them both for a very long time.

"Let's talk about that perfume," he said.

"I know I wasn't supposed to touch it. I wanted to remember what Mama smelled like."

"I want to remember too," Daddy said. "But that bottle is very precious and you mustn't touch it without my permission."

Calvin jumped off his lap. Clara knew he'd been sitting too long and needed to run around. He wasn't very good at sitting in one place for more than a minute. He picked up some of the Cheerios from the floor and hid them in his fist.

"Whoa, there, little guy." Daddy brushed Calvin's hand into the sink and scooped up the rest of the cereal on the floor and tossed it in the garbage. "No Cheerios for you until your mouth has a rest. Let's go and build a fort." He took Calvin's hand and they walked into the living room together, leaving Clara alone.

Clara didn't know what to do. She'd told the truth and still Daddy went to play with Calvin. She felt like kicking down Calvin's garage wall. It seemed Daddy only noticed someone's feelings when they threw a tantrum, like Calvin did.

Did Daddy *really* like him best?

10

Clara squinted at the clock on the dashboard of the car. 7:10. The dance recital started at 7:30. She kept hoping Daddy would drive faster.

Ten minutes ago, she hadn't known if they'd ever get there. Calvin couldn't find Poppy. He'd cried and said he wouldn't go without him. Clara and Daddy searched everywhere. Finally, they found Poppy in the bathroom cupboard, behind the toilet paper. They were in such a hurry, Daddy hadn't asked how Poppy had got there. He'd wrapped Calvin in a coat and whisked him and the bear out to the car, with Clara running behind.

Everything was disorganized because Tess was

writing an exam that night. She'd left everything they needed in a pile on the counter. Before she left, she'd fixed Clara's hair in a bun, because Daddy didn't know how to do it. "Make sure you record your dance," she had said, "and I'll watch it on Monday." Clara wished that Tess could have come too, and she wished that everything didn't go wrong when Tess was away. Like losing Poppy.

Now she worried that they'd be late. Miss Tabitha would be so mad. Clara had practiced her routine for weeks and finally learned the steps.

When they reached the school Daddy said, "The show begins in fifteen minutes. I'll drop you off at the front door. Can you find your way backstage while we park the car?"

Clara nodded, even though she wasn't sure. She was late already and didn't want to waste any time. Luckily, when she got into the school, signs were taped up everywhere. She followed them and ran down the hall to the changing room.

"You're late, Clara," Miss Tabitha said. "I still have to put on your makeup. Where's your costume?"

Costume? Clara looked around the room at nine other girls in beige skirts. She gulped.

"Um, I think my dad has it."

"Is your father in the audience?" Miss Tabitha asked.

"No, he's parking the car."

"Then we'll begin with your makeup. You can get your costume when I'm finished."

Miss Tabitha asked Clara to stop fidgeting three times while she was putting on her makeup. Clara watched the clock race toward 7:30. Would Miss Tabitha ever be done? The other girls were dressed and made up, waiting. Jenny was telling one of her jokes, and everyone was laughing.

"There," Miss Tabitha said, setting down the lipstick. "Run and get your costume. We're on in five minutes."

Clara rushed out to the gym. She stopped at the door. The gym was packed with people, most of them taller than her. How would she ever find Daddy?

She walked down the centre aisle searching row by row, left and right. If only Calvin were crying now, at least she'd hear where they were.

She found them in the second row from the back. "What are you doing here?" Daddy asked. "Aren't you dancing in a few minutes?"

"Yeah, but I need my costume."

"Costume?"

"You brought it, right?" Clara asked.

Daddy's face went pale. "Are you positive you didn't bring it? It might be in the car." He stood up.

Clara shook her head. "I didn't think about it either."

The lights were dimming. He ran his hand through his hair. "It must be sitting on the counter. I could go home and get it."

"There isn't time. We're dancing third."

"I'm sorry, Clara. I don't know what else to do."

She felt a lump in her throat. "I'll ask Miss Tabitha."

She ran back up the centre aisle, down the hall, and into the changing room where the rest of the class was already lining up. Miss Tabitha frowned when she saw that Clara still had no costume.

"We left it at home," Clara said. She was trying not to cry, but she felt a hot tear splash out of her left eye and run down her cheek. She dug her fingernails into her hands to stop crying.

"Don't cry or you'll ruin your makeup," Miss Tabitha said, dabbing at Clara's face with a tissue. "I don't have any extra costumes. You'll have to go on like that. You won't stand out as much if you move to the right side, next to Ashley."

Clara took her place in line. She was standing behind Jenny now. "I'm sorry," Jenny said, squeezing Clara's hand.

"And for heaven's sake, Clara, point your toes," Miss Tabitha said.

Miss Tabitha had moved Ashley to the back row after March Break because of her broken arm. Her cast was off now, but she was still in the back. She glared as Clara moved in beside her, but didn't say anything.

As the second group began their dance, Miss Tabitha's helper, Miss Dawn, helped arrange everyone in straight lines. Clara watched the other girls in her class, all of them dressed in the little beige skirts that twirled. Clara looked down at her black, stretchy pants and blue hoodie. She dug her nails into her palms again.

"Be alert, girls. You're on next," Miss Tabitha said.

The other group filed off the stage, and Clara's class walked on. The bright lights shone in her eyes, so she couldn't see the audience. She already knew how many people were in the gym — a lot.

Clara pointed her toe to the side. She heard someone in the audience giggling. She wished she hadn't gone on the stage.

Why hadn't Daddy remembered her costume? He'd been too busy looking for Poppy. Why did he act like Calvin was more important than her?

The music began. She still hated "Be Prepared," and tonight it was worse than ever. Every time Scar sang the words "Be prepared," Clara's face burned. *She* hadn't been prepared, and now she was dancing out of costume.

Everyone was probably looking at her, thinking, "Why isn't that dancer prepared?"

The dance had never seemed so long. The music was playing slower than ever before. She wanted to run off the stage and hide under one of the desks in the changing room.

Mama had come last year, even though she was really sick and had to leave right after Clara's dance. Maybe this year Mama's spirit was watching her. Mama wouldn't care if she was wearing the wrong clothes.

But if Mama were alive, she would have remembered Clara's costume.

Clara's mind came back to the dance. Ashley was hissing beside her. As Clara lowered her right arm, she noticed the others lowering their left arms. How long had she been out of step?

"Be prepared," Scar sang again. Clara closed her eyes for a second and wished she was anywhere else.

Finally the dance was over. The music ended, and the girls ran off the stage. Miss Tabitha and Miss Dawn were waiting for them in the hall.

"Well done! I'd like to take your pictures before you change," Miss Tabitha said. "Pose against the wall. Return to the formation that you danced in." She glanced at Clara. "You can be in the picture if you want, but lean down behind Jenny." The girls gathered in two lines.

Ashley rolled her eyes at Clara. "Why are you always wrecking things?" she asked. "You messed up that dance — again. And everyone else remembered their costumes. Why didn't you?"

11

Ashley glared at Clara. "Why did you bother getting a costume if you weren't going to wear it?" Ashley said.

Clara looked around. Miss Tabitha and Miss Dawn weren't paying attention. Ashley was careful to be mean only when no adults were listening.

"Miss Tabitha said —" Clara stopped herself. She had almost told Ashley that Miss Tabitha had asked her to wear her blue hoodie. But she wasn't going to lie anymore.

Jenny turned around. "Don't pay any attention to Ashley," she whispered. "I forget things sometimes, too."

Clara remembered what Jenny had said on the snow day: *She used to be mean to me, but I ignored her. And she stopped.*

Maybe I should just ignore her, Clara thought. But ignoring her wouldn't be enough. She wouldn't forget all of the mean things Ashley had said to her, and Ashley needed to know it was wrong.

What if she stood up to her? Ashley couldn't be any *more* mean than she already was. And Clara was tired of being afraid of her. She couldn't change everything in her life. She might not be able to get Mama back, or get out of dance class, but she wasn't going to let Ashley scare her anymore.

"I don't like it when you boss me. I want you to leave me alone," Clara said.

Jenny gasped. Stephanie's head swung round to face Clara, and her eyes were big and round.

Clara continued. "I think you should be nicer to people. Not just to me, but everyone."

Clara waited for Ashley to say something mean. But Ashley shrugged. "Whatever," she said.

Miss Tabitha rejoined the group. "I'm all set,"

she said, holding the camera up. "Say cheese!" But before taking the picture she lowered her arms. "For heaven's sake, Ashley, did you swallow a lemon? Smile!"

The flash went off and Clara's eyes blinked with the light. The girls broke out of their formation, and Jenny spun and giggled. "You were awesome," she said.

Clara grinned. "Thanks," she said.

"Miss Dawn, can you wait with the girls until my next class is finished?" Miss Tabitha called. "When they're done dancing, we'll all go to the changing room together."

As Miss Tabitha went backstage, the gym door opened and Mrs. Singh walked into the hall. Most of the girls who were in her class at school rushed over to say hi, but Clara hung back. She was hoping that Mrs. Singh wouldn't see her. She didn't want to talk to anyone while she was wearing her stupid stretch pants.

But Mrs. Singh caught her eye. "There you are, Clara," she said, coming over.

"You saw our dance?" Clara asked.

"I wouldn't have missed it for the world."

Clara glanced away. Mrs. Singh must think she wasn't a real dancer. "I forgot my costume at home," she said. "I guess I looked funny on the stage."

Mrs. Singh sounded surprised. "Usually the star wears a different costume than the rest of the company. I thought you were dressed like that on purpose."

Clara looked up at Mrs. Singh, who winked at her. *She knows I forgot my outfit, and she doesn't care. She still likes me and she's trying to make me feel better.* Clara smiled back. "Thanks, Mrs. Singh," she said.

The music got louder for a minute as the gym door opened again. Daddy and Calvin came out, blinking in the bright hall.

Mrs. Singh hugged Clara. "You'll want to talk to your dad. I'll see you on Monday." She walked back into the gym as Clara ran to greet Daddy.

She rushed into his arms. "Hey, you were great!" he said. "I can tell you've been practicing."

Calvin reached out and tugged Clara's hoodie.

"I'm sorry about your costume," Daddy said. "But you looked great up there. You were the best dancer in your class."

Clara couldn't keep it in any longer. "No I'm not! I'm the worst." She saw Daddy's eyes open in surprise. "And don't say it isn't true, because it is!"

"I know you're feeling disappointed about the costume. I would be too. But in a few days, I think you'll feel pretty good about the recital."

Clara stood in front of Daddy and put her hands on her hips. "I'm a terrible dancer, and I hate ballet."

Daddy frowned. "Clara, you don't mean that."

"Yes, I do." Clara swallowed hard. Now was the time for Daddy to be angry. Of course he wouldn't understand. He wanted Clara to be in ballet as much as Mama had. Would she have to stay in dance class for the rest of her life?

Daddy tilted his head to the side. "I had no idea you didn't like it. Why didn't you say something before?"

He didn't seem mad. He looked surprised.

Maybe she still had a chance to tell him. "I tried, Daddy, but you fell asleep. And the other times — you just seemed too sad."

Calvin galloped away down the hall. Daddy watched him go but didn't run after him. He knelt beside Clara and took her hand. "Sometimes it makes me sad to remember Mama, but I love talking about her with you and Calvin. No one loved her more than the three of us, right?"

Clara shook her head. "No one."

"I haven't been fair to you. Your mother was a wonderful dancer, and I guess I expected you to follow in her footsteps. You have your own talents and I want you to follow them."

"Really?" Clara's eyes were glowing. She felt like Daddy had taken a huge lump out of her throat.

"And I want you to feel like you can talk to me anytime, about anything that's on your mind."

Clara took a deep breath. Now was the time to ask her other big question. "Daddy?"

"Yes, sweetie?"

"Do you love me as much as you love Calvin?"

"Clara!"

She hung her head. "You always pick Calvin instead of me. When he spilled his orange juice, you changed him and let Tess help me. You bought Calvin new clothes this winter, but didn't buy me anything until Tess got mad at you. You even made me late tonight because we were looking for Calvin's bear."

The music stopped and there was a burst of applause from the gym. A group of green ballerinas trampled their way into the hall.

Daddy's eyes filled with tears. "I love you so much, Clara. Maybe I understand Calvin more because he's a boy. And he's younger than you, so he needs to be watched more closely. But that doesn't mean you don't need me." Calvin galloped back and landed in a heap beside Clara and Daddy. Daddy reached down to ruffle his hair, but kept talking to Clara. "Let's make a promise to each other. I'll always be there for you, and you'll come to me any time you need to talk. Deal?"

"Deal," Clara said.

The two classes of girls skipped back to the changing room. Stephanie grinned at her on the way by. Jenny stopped and hugged Clara. Ashley caught Clara's eye for a second, but looked away.

"You were brave to dance," Jenny said. "I'm glad you did."

"You're right about Ashley. I don't think she'll bug me anymore."

Jenny lowered her voice. "I wonder if it would work with Miss Tabitha, too." The girls laughed.

"Hey guess what? Lexy's mom is handing out popsicles in the changing room," Jenny continued. "Let's go!"

"I'm just talking to my dad for a minute. I'll meet you when we're done."

"I want one," Calvin said.

"There's tons of them, Mr. Cooper," Jenny said. "Can I take Calvin?"

"That would be great," Daddy said. "Thanks."

"No problem. I'll bring him back in a sec." Jenny took Calvin by the hand and led him down the hall, holding Poppy under her free arm. Clara hoped Calvin hadn't slobbered on Poppy. There was nothing worse than carrying a stuffed animal that Calvin had chewed, unless it was a stuffed animal that he'd wiped his nose on.

Some of the kids were in the hall with popsicles in their mouths, and the muffled sound of "The Circle of Life" drifted out of the gym. Daddy pointed to an empty classroom with the door partially open. "It might be a little quieter if we went in there," he said.

The two of them walked into the empty room. Daddy lifted Clara to sit on the teacher's desk, and he leaned against it. "I was thinking about what you said the other day. About remembering Mama."

"I think about Mama every day. I don't ever want to stop."

"I don't either." Daddy took her hand. "Tell me one thing you remember."

"When she tucked me in at bedtime, she always sang "Toora Loora Loora.""

"When you were a baby, she held you in the rocking chair and sang that lullaby until you fell asleep. She loved you so much."

Clara held her breath. It meant a lot to hear how Mama loved her. When Daddy talked about Mama, Clara didn't want to say a word. She just wanted to listen.

He reached in his coat pocket and drew out a small, red gift bag painted with gold swirls. It reminded Clara of Mama's Valentine's Day scarf. "This is my gift to you," he said. "I hope it helps you remember Mama."

Clara pulled out a wad of tissue paper with something heavy inside. She carefully peeled the tissue paper until the gift was open.

Daddy had given her a perfume bottle. It was clear, with tiny flowers etched into the sides.

"Roses for Mama," Clara said. She ran her thumb along the side and felt the ridges. It didn't look like Mama's bottle, but it was almost as beautiful.

"Keep this on your dresser, and I'll fill it with her perfume. That way you can smell it whenever you want to remember her."

Clara's heart was so full, she couldn't say a word.

"And when you're older, I'll give you hers."
Daddy leaned over and looked right into her eyes.
"Clara, I'm not perfect. Sometimes I make mistakes, like forgetting your ballet costume, or giving you boys' clothes to try on. But don't ever forget how much I love you."

Clara cradled the bottle gently. For the first time in a long time, she didn't feel like she had to invent anything. She had everything she needed.